characters created by

lauren child

HELP!
I really mean it!

Grosset & Dunlap

Text based on the script written by Anna Starkey

Illustrations from the TV animation produced by Tiger Aspect

GROSSET & DUNLAP
Published by the Penguin Group
Penguin Group (USA) Inc., 375 Hudson Street, New York, New York 10014, USA
Penguin Group (Canada), 90 Eglinton Avenue East, Suite 700, Toronto, Ontario M4P 2Y3, Canada
(a division of Pearson Penguin Canada Inc.)
Penguin Books Ltd., 80 Strand, London WC2R 0RL, England
Penguin Group Ireland, 25 St. Stephen's Green, Dublin 2, Ireland
(a division of Penguin Books Ltd.)
Penguin Group (Australia), 250 Camberwell Road, Camberwell, Victoria 3124, Australia
(a division of Pearson Australia Group Pty. Ltd.)
Penguin Books India Pvt. Ltd., 11 Community Centre, Panchsheel Park, New Delhi—110 017, India
Penguin Group (NZ), 67 Apollo Drive, Rosedale, North Shore 0632, New Zealand
(a division of Pearson New Zealand Ltd.)
Penguin Books (South Africa) (Pty.) Ltd., 24 Sturdee Avenue,
Rosebank, Johannesburg 2196, South Africa

Penguin Books Ltd., Registered Offices: 80 Strand, London WC2R 0RL, England

Library of Congress Cataloging-in-Publication Data is available.

ISBN 978-0-448-45049-0   10 9 8 7 6 5 4 3 2 1

I have this little sister, Lola.
She is small and very funny.
Today we are looking after Caspar,
Granny and Grandpa's cat.
Lola REALLY loves Caspar.

Lola says,
    "Look, Charlie!
Caspar is playing
    a game with us."

So I say,
    "Caspar is a cat.
        He might not like
    all of your games."

"He definitely
likes this one," says Lola.

Then Lola says,
"Lotta, did you know
        that Caspar is an
    actual tiger..."

"Oooh! Lola,
what are those noises?"
                    asks Lotta.

Lola says,
            "I don't know.
But it's all right because
    we are with Caspar.

Oh . . .
        where's Caspar gone?"

And Lotta says, "Oh! Yes!
    Where's Caspar gone?"

Then Lola and Lotta shout,
    "HEEEELLLLPPPPP!"

Me and Marv run in
        and ask,
        "Are you all right?!"

And Lola says,
        "Yes, Charlie!
        Caspar was just going to
rescue me and Lotta
        from some tigers."

So I say,
"Lola, you must ONLY
        call for help
if you REALLY mean it."

And Lola says,
"Sorry, Charlie.
        We only said HELP
by accident."

Lotta says,
"It was very funny
when we said HELP
and Charlie and Marv
came running in."

And Lola asks,
"Do you think
if we say help now,
they will come in
again?"

"HELP! HELP!
HELP! HELP!"

"What's the matter?!"
        me and Marv ask.

And Lola says,
        "Nothing, Charlie . . ."

So I say,
        "Oh. I get it.
        Very funny."

"We won't do it again,"
says Lola.

        So I ask,
        "Do you promise?"

        And Lola says,
"We absolutely
        do promise."

Later Lotta says,
    "Look! Caspar
likes **dressing up**.

Do you think **cats**
like wearing **hats**?"

"Oh! I know they do,"
    says Lola.
"And they like going
for **carriage rides**, too.

Come on, Caspar.
    It's time for a **ride**."

"Caspar, where are you?"

"Are you here, Caspar?"
"Caspar! Where are you?"

"Caspar!
CASPAR!"

And I ask, "What is it
           this time, Lola?"

Lola says,
"Caspar's stuck
           right up in the sky,
and he's crying and his
           hat's gone all **wonky!**"

So I say,
           "Sorry, Lola.
It's not going to
           work this time."

And Lola says,
"But Charlie,
           we really, REALLY
need you to **help** . . ."

"Charlie and Marv
don't believe me
so we've got to get Caspar
down by ourselves.
Please come down, Caspar!"

And Lotta says, "PLEASE!"

Then Caspar climbs
higher up the tree.

And Lola shouts,
"Noooooo!
Charlie! HELP!"

Me and Marv run over
and Lola says,
"See? I did **really** need you."

And I say, "But I didn't
believe you because
you kept **shouting** HELP
when you didn't mean it."

Lola and Lotta say,
"Sorry, Charlie.
Sorry, Marv."

And I say,
"Look! Caspar has **jumped**
onto Marv's balcony!"

Then Marv says, "Err . . . Charlie,
why is that **cat** wearing a **hat**?"

So I say, "**Cats** don't like **hats**, Lola."

And Marv says,
"I would run away, too, if I had to wear a **hat** like that!"